Loudmouth Louis

Anne Fine was born and educated in the Midlands, and now lives in County Durham. She has written numerous highly acclaimed and prize-winning books for children and adults.

Her novel *Goggle-Eyes* won the *Guardian* Children's Fiction Award and the Carnegie Medal, and was adapted for television by the BBC; *Flour Babies* won the Carnegie Medal and the Whitbread Children's Novel Award; *Bill's New Frock* won a Smarties Award; *Madame Doubtfire* has become a major feature film by Twentieth-Century Fox, starring Robin Williams, and, most recently, *The Tulip Touch* was the winner of the Whitbread Children's Book of the Year Award for 1996.

Some other books by Anne Fine

Books for Younger Readers

CARE OF HENRY
COUNTDOWN
DESIGN-A-PRAM
THE DIARY OF A KILLER CAT
THE HAUNTING OF PIP PARKER
JENNIFER'S DIARY
ONLY A SHOW
PRESS PLAY
THE SAME OLD STORY EVERY YEAR
SCAREDY-CAT
STRANGER DANGER?
THE WORST CHILD I EVER HAD

Books for Middle Range Readers

THE ANGEL OF NITSHILL ROAD
ANNELI THE ART HATER
BILL'S NEW FROCK
THE CHICKEN GAVE IT TO ME
THE COUNTRY PANCAKE
CRUMMY MUMMY AND ME
HOW TO WRITE REALLY BADLY
A PACK OF LIARS
A SUDDEN GLOW OF GOLD
A SUDDEN PUFF OF GLITTERING SMOKE
A SUDDEN SWIRL OF ICY WIND

ANNE FINE

Loudmouth Louis

Illustrated by Kate Aldous

PUFFIN BOOKS

PUFFIN BOOKS

Published by the Penguin Group
Penguin Books Ltd, 27 Wrights Lane, London W8 5TZ, England
Penguin Putnam Inc., 375 Hudson Street, New York, New York 10014, USA
Penguin Books Australia Ltd, Ringwood, Victoria, Australia
Penguin Books Canada Ltd, 10 Alcorn Avenue, Toronto, Ontario, Canada M4V 3B2
Penguin Books (NZ) Ltd, Private Bag 102902, NSMC, Auckland, New Zealand

Penguin Books Ltd, Registered Offices: Harmondsworth, Middlesex, England

First published 1998
5 7 9 10 8 6

Text copyright © Anne Fine, 1998
Illustrations copyright © Kate Aldous, 1998
All rights reserved

The moral right of the author and illustrator has been asserted

Typeset in Monotype Baskerville

Made and printed in England by Clays Ltd, St Ives plc

British Library Cataloguing in Publication Data
A CIP catalogue record for this book is available from the British Library

ISBN 0–141–30205–4

Contents

1   Silence is Golden   1

2   Fifty Different Ways to be
Told to be Quiet   4

3   Worry on My Mind   9

4   Don't Mind My Dad   14

5   In Training   21

6   A New Manager   27

7   Sponsorship   29

8   Fresh Start, Fresh Colours   40

9   Interesting . . .   44

10   Fly on the Wall   72

1 Silence is Golden

IT WAS MY own fault, I admit.

I could have been in the group that chose to organize the Raffle. But I was too busy chatting to Melanie to bother to put up my hand.

And I could have joined the group Miss Sparkes said could run the Bring-And-Buy Stall. But I was leaning across to whisper something to George, so I missed that chance too.

And then Steve and Arif and Arianne finally persuaded Miss Sparkes to let them run a Who-Can-Have-Wet-Sponges-Thrown-At-Them-Longest

Competition. And I'd have joined up
with them, but she was still mad at me
for chattering in class, so she wouldn't
put my name down.

She just set her timer as usual.

"Silence is golden, Louis Todd," she

said. "If you can button your loud mouth for five whole minutes, I'll write your name down. And if you can't, I won't."

I couldn't. So she didn't.

So I was still sulking when she wrote down the names of people who wanted to do the Biscuit-Making. And the Guess-The-Number-Of-Lollipops-In-The-Jar. And the Great-Big-Used-Book Sale.

The trouble is, I was *still* sulking when she asked if I wanted to join the very last group, who were going to set up the Fast-Cheapo-Car-Wash.

"No, thanks," I told her. "I have a brilliant idea of my own to make some money. And it's *private*."

"That's nice," she said. (You could tell she was pleased that I wouldn't have to discuss it with anyone.) "And now it's time for Maths."

So, as I told you, it was all my own fault.

2 Fifty Different Ways
to be Told to be Quiet

I AM THE world's expert in being told to be quiet. Everyone has their own way of doing it. I know, because I get it all day.

In the morning, Mum stares at me blearily over her cornflakes. "There's no point in talking to me yet, Louis," she says. "Can't you see that I'm still asleep?"

When we're leaving the house, Dad claps his hand over my mouth. "Hush up, Louis. Just give me a moment to think if there's anything I've forgotten."

At the lollipop crossing, Mrs Frier says, "Louis Todd, you rattle on like a stone in a tin can."

The big boys in the playground say, "Stuff it!" or "Shut your cakehole!" or "Belt up!" or "Stow it!" (In case you're tempted, I should warn you that my mother says if she ever, *ever* hears me say any one of those again, all I'll get for Christmas is a freshly spanked bottom.)

In Assembly, Mrs Heap says, "Is that Louis Todd I hear talking?" Or, sometimes, "I take it that what you're saying, Louis Todd, is a whole lot more important than what I'm saying. So why don't you come up here and tell it to everyone?"

(That shuts me up pretty sharpish.)

Back in the classroom, Miss Sparkes says, one by one, through the long morning:

"Stop talking, Louis."

"Be quiet, please."

"That's enough, Mr Loudmouth."

"Louis, I'm *speaking*."

"Do stop distracting other people."

"I don't recall saying you could work in pairs."

At lunch-time, the dinner ladies stand right over me, and say things like, "Give over prattling, Louis Todd, and finish your sponge pudding." Or "Stop rabbiting on and *eat*. Can't you see that we're waiting to get on and wipe this table?"

After lunch, back in the classroom, Miss Sparkes starts up again.

"Don't start nattering."

"I'm sick and tired of hearing your voice, Louis."

"I think *Ben* was talking."

"I'll put on my timer, and see how long Loudmouth Louis can keep his beak buttoned."

"Don't interrupt me. Zip your lip, please, Louis."

"On your own, please."

When we're learning about other countries, she sometimes says it in other languages.

"*Tais-toi!*" (That's French.)

"*¡Cállate!*" (Spanish.)

"ચુપ રે" (Gujarati.)

By the end of the day, she's usually digging in her bag for her aspirins. "Louis, you realize that you've given me another splitting headache."

Once, she was so fed up, she even said, as I was going out of the door, "I shall know when you're dead, shan't I, Louis Todd? It'll go nice and quiet."

After all that, it's lovely to get home to Gran.

3 *Worry on My Mind*

GRAN NEVER TELLS me off for talking. Well, she can't. She's just as bad herself.

Gran never stops. When we're together in the house, it's her voice stirring up the air, not mine.

Gran even talks when no one's there to listen. I can walk home from school, push open the door, and hear her at it.

". . . so I'll just wash these dishes to get them out of the way, and then sort out that peg basket. Yes, here's a couple of broken ones I can throw straight in the

9

bin. And now I'll have a look at this
tea towel and see if it's due for a wash
yet . . ."

Mum calls it "chuntering", and says that
toddlers do it. Ask a small child to get
dressed, says Mum, and suddenly there in
front of you is a strangely bulging heap
that's trying to tell you things.

". . . now I'm putting on my woolly
and, *whoops,* got *stuck,* and it's all gone

dark, and I can't find the *hole,* and now all the *rest* of me's stuck too, and I can't find my way out, and . . ."

Mum says that chuntering is useful practice if you're learning to talk. But you ought to grow out of it. Obviously, Gran's grown back into it again, because I've heard most of the things she's said eight million times before.

"There! Now the kitchen's looking

fresh and tidy. And when your mum and dad get home after a hard day's work, I think it's nice for them not to have to walk into a bomb-site."

But sometimes what she says is news to me.

"See that bald man on the front of the telly guide, Louis? Well, when he was young, he had lovely thick curls and he looked like an upside-down floor mop."

But I wasn't interested in bald men, or fresh and tidy kitchens. I had a worry on my mind.

"Gran," I said. "Today I did something really stupid. I didn't sign on to help with washing cars or making biscuits."

"Sounds smart to me," said Gran. "Sit with your feet up and let other people do the work."

"The trouble is," I said, "that I told Miss Sparkes I had my own brilliant idea to make some money."

"That's good," said Gran. "My Dance Club needs some money. I hope you won't mind sharing your idea with me."

"I would," I said, "except I haven't had it yet."

"Pity," said Gran. "Because all of us in the Dance Club want to go to Blackpool and stay in the Alhambra, and walk along the sea front, and go to the Tower Ballroom every night, and –"

So it was too late. I had missed my chance.

4 Don't Mind My Dad

I tried talking to her again later. Dad wasn't listening. He was slumped on the sofa watching *Leighton Buzzard Wanderers' Greatest Goals*. Dad watches football videos for half an hour after he gets home. Gran tells him off. But Dad says if she'd had forty little savages yelling at her all day, she'd sit and watch *Leighton Buzzard Wanderers' Greatest Goals* with him.

(My dad's a teacher. Did I mention that?)

"Gran," I said. "About this brilliant idea I need for making money . . ."

14

She had a think.

"You could put lots of lollipops in a jar," she said. "And make people pay to guess how many there are."

"Someone's already doing that," I told her.

"Sssh!" Dad's voice came up from the sofa. "Here comes the first of Lenny Potter's unforgettable match-savers."

"Well, then," Gran said to me. "How about setting up a Great-Big-Used-Book Sale?"

"That's been picked too," I said.

On the television, Lenny Potter took a penalty back in the stone age when Leighton Buzzard Wanderers wore those old yellow shirts with purple stripes.

"A pity about that nasty rash of his," Gran fretted.

"Sssh!" Dad said.

I said, "He doesn't look as if he has a rash to me."

"That was back then," said Gran. "When he was young and fit. I saw him last night on *A Question of Sport* and he'd come up in pink lumps."

Dad raised his head over the rim of the sofa.

"Instead of joining the two of you to grieve over the poor man's skin problems," he said, "might I just be permitted to watch his famous left-footed

volley from the halfway line in peace and quiet?"

(Don't mind my dad. Like Mrs Heap, he can be very sarcastic.)

"Sad, too, about his poor wife . . ." persisted Gran.

"Sssh!" Dad said. "This is the corner kick that flew in above the great, late Juan Da Silva like a bird."

"Her big mistake, of course," said Gran, "was leaving a fine man like him to marry that bear."

"She married a *bear*?"

Gran gave me a very pitying look and turned back to Dad.

"What was his name, Brian? Giant great lump of a fellow who wore floppy bow ties and knew a lot about furniture. Always on *Antiques Roadshow*. You remember!"

Dad huddled closer to the television as Lenny Potter, now in a purple shirt with yellow stripes, booted the ball all the way from the hot-dog stand to the entrance to the Ladies. He had his fingers in his ears. (Dad. Not Lenny Potter.)

"Gran!" I reminded her. "About this brilliant idea I need for making money for school . . ."

Dad's head came back over the sofa. "What does your school need money for now?"

"For the new library."

He sank back down. "That's all right then," he told me. "Someone like you needn't feel bad about not raising any. They'd never let you in anyway. Libraries are quiet places."

"I can be quiet when I want."

"And pigs can fly."

He went back to watching his video. Gran could see that my feelings were hurt.

"You could always run a Raffle," she

suggested. "Or even a Bring-And-Buy
Stall." Her eyes lit up. "I could give you
those nice socks with dancing Santas to
take in, since your father won't –"

"Sssh!" Dad said. "You're talking
through that great direct free-kick that
sailed in on a perfect curve."

"The Raffle and the Bring-And-Buy
Stall are both being done already," I told
Gran. "And so is the Who-Can-Have-

Wet-Sponges-Thrown-At-Them-Longest Competition."

"People don't want wet sponges thrown at them, Louis," Gran said. "What people want is useful things, like having their cars cleaned cheaply. Or nice things, like home-made biscuits."

She leaned over the sofa.

"You wouldn't pay to have wet sponges thrown at you, would you, Brian?"

"No," Dad said. "But I'd give quite a lot of money to be able to sit and watch my video in peace and quiet."

Gran didn't even hear him. But I did.

5 In Training

SO THAT'S HOW the brilliant idea was born. Louis Todd's Great Sponsored Silence.

First, I had to get in training. On Monday, I tried to keep quiet all the way back from Assembly to the classroom. I got as far as the turn in the corridor. Then Lucy said, "Louis –" And I said, "What?"

So that was thirteen seconds.

I had another go back in the classroom.

"I want everyone to be quiet while I give out the measuring kits," said Miss

Sparkes. "And that includes you, Louis."

So I was quiet.

Ten seconds.

Twenty.

Thirty.

And then, "I don't want that one," I told her. "That one's got bits missing."

Thirty-one seconds. If you're generous. Not very good.

I tried again during Percussion Band. I reckoned that there'd be so much noise going on around me that I could probably give my own voice a rest a bit more easily.

How wrong I was.

First, Mr Hambleton gave me the cowbells to hand out. I gave the first to Melanie (in perfect silence).

Ten seconds. Looking good!

I gave the second to Marisa (in silence too).

Fifteen seconds.

And then I gave the last one to Alfie. "There you go," I said. "Cowbell. It suits you."

I hadn't kept counting, but it wasn't a record. It would have been eighteen seconds at most.

I gave up for the rest of the class. I like Percussion Band, and keeping quiet when you can hardly be heard over the bongos and chime bars and woodblocks and triangles is pretty much a waste of time. So I only tried again when it was time to collect up the tambourines.

I didn't speak as I walked round the circle, taking them. But, as I passed George, I couldn't help giving all four a jolly good rattle, and saying, "*¡Olé!*"

So that was pretty much a waste of effort. (Back to ten seconds at most.)

*

On the way home, I walked by myself as far as the lollipop crossing. Forty-two seconds.

Then Mrs Frier said, "Why are you staring at your watch, Louis? Are you late for something?"

"No," I said.

Forty-six seconds. Not an impressive record. I was so fed up, I walked home

with Emma and talked to her non-stop
about Leighton Buzzard Wanderers.

Give up on training for today, I thought,
as I walked through the door. No point
in trying in the same house as Gran. But
I was wrong. As soon as I explained what
I was doing, she started rooting through
one of the kitchen drawers.

"What are you looking for?"

"Sticky tape." She held it up. "Just a few inches over your mouth. Trust me, it'll work a treat."

And so it did, till Dad came home, and Gran explained.

Dad peeled the tape off.

"Don't think that poor Miss Sparkes hasn't dreamed of doing this," he said. "She'd probably even be happy to pay for the sticky tape out of the money she'd save on her aspirins. But I'm afraid it's not allowed."

"But if I've agreed . . ."

Dad shook his head sadly. "Just forget it, son. I am a teacher and I know. Leave her to *dream*."

And he slid in his video.

6 A New Manager

WHEN MUM CAME home, she found me crying at the bottom of the stairs.

"What's all this?"

"Nothing," I snivelled.

"Come off it, Louis. Something's wrong. Tell me."

She pulled me on her knee, and I explained about the sponsored silence, and the sticky tape Gran put on my mouth, and not being able to keep quiet without it.

Mum patted me gently. "What you need," she said, "is a new manager."

I wiped away my tears. "What, like

Leighton Buzzard Wanderers?"

"That's right."

"But, *who*?"

"Who do you think?" Mum said, grinning. "Me, of course."

7 Sponsorship

THE FIRST THING we did was go after sponsorship. I made out the form.

NAME	AMOUNT PER HOUR	MAXIMUM
May Todd	20p	£1.50
Brian Todd	20p	£1.50
Mrs Havergill	10p	£1.00

In the first column, you put your name. In the next, you wrote how much you wanted to pay for each hour I kept quiet. And at the end you had to write the most you would give, even if I never spoke again.

"That's only fair," said Mum. "After all, you might have a terrible fright, and be struck dumb for ever."

("No such luck!" Dad said.)

First, I went round to Mrs Havergill next door, just for the practice.

"Please, Mrs Havergill, will you sponsor me to keep quiet all Friday?"

"How much is it?" she asked me.

"You get to choose," I said.

She looked me up and down. "Ten pence an hour? And a pound maximum? What a pity you're not doing a Saturday!"

She wrote her name down. I rushed back to Mum.

"It works! It works!"

"Only if you keep quiet," she reminded me. "But we'll leave that problem for now. One step at a time."

*

Next day, I took my form into school.
Everyone was thrilled.

Miss Sparkes put herself down for fifty
pence an hour.

"Cheap at *double* the price!" she told
me. Her eyes gleamed. "And if it works,
we'll do it again. Over and over! Why
stop at a new library? We could have a
new music centre. And a new sports
stadium. You could be quiet every day,
all term, until you're out of my class!"

I gave her my hurt look.

"Oh, all right," she said. "We'll just see
how it goes on Friday, shall we?"

Snatching the form from me, she
signed her name.

All of my friends signed up. And lots of
other people I hadn't realized I'd been
bothering.

"Does this mean you'll be quiet all

through Reading Time? If you will, I'll pay. When you keep interrupting in Reading, we never get to the end of the story, and I hate that."

"Is there any chance you'll be able to stay quiet all through Maths Workbook? Then I might get to understand subtraction, and that would be *brilliant*."

"How much is it to sponsor you all through Gym Class? Then we might get to use the ropes for once. I love it when everyone's quiet, and we get to use the ropes."

"I'll pay if you promise to try extra hard all through *Pictures from History* on the telly. I love *Pictures from History*, but when you're talking, I can't hear."

The dinner ladies laughed and laughed.

"You? Loudmouth Louis Todd? Stay quiet for even one hour? One whole *hour*?"

"I'm aiming for the whole day."

"Oh, yes?" Both of them laughed some more.

"I should warn you," I said, "I'm under new management, so it could happen."

"And Leighton Buzzard Wanderers could win the Cup!"

They fell about laughing some more. Then Mrs James put out her hand. "Give me your form, and I'll sign up."

She did. And so did Mrs Patel. I looked to see what they'd written.

£1,000,000 an hour, Mrs James had put. *Maximum £5,000,000.*

And Mrs Patel had written *Ditto* underneath.

Off they went, laughing.

Then I went after Mrs Heap, who was striding down the corridor. "Please will you sponsor me for the new library?"

"Sponsor you to do what, Louis?"

"Keep quiet."

She stopped in her tracks. "What? Not talk? For a whole hour?"

"For a whole day, if I can."

"You? Louis Todd?" She laid a hand over my forehead. "Are you feverish?"

"No," I said. "I'm determined. I'm under new management, like Leighton Buzzard Wanderers. And I shall do it."

She seized my form. "Louis," she said, writing busily. "If you can keep quiet for a whole school day, I shall be very tempted to put up a plaque to commemorate the occasion."

"A real plaque? Oh, excellent! What would it say?"

She tilted her head to one side. "Well, if you're going to make a lot of money, how about: *Silence was Golden*?"

I whistled through my teeth. "*Magic!*"

Mrs Heap gave me a beady look.

"Yes," she said. "Magic. And that's what you're going to need to get you through the first five minutes."

She handed the form back, and away she went.

Next stop, Mr Hambleton.

"Sponsor me, please, for shutting up?"

"Shutting up?" The same light gleamed in his eyes as in Miss Sparkes'. "What? All through Percussion Band?"

"I *would*," I said. "Except that Percussion Band isn't till next Monday, and I'm doing this Friday."

"I'll get the timetable changed," he cried. "I'll go after Mrs Heap right now, and make her do it. This is an opportunity not to be missed!"

He snatched the form, and scribbled on it madly.

"A whole Percussion Band practice without you talking! Oh, it's too good to

be true! I can hardly wait! Roll on, Friday! And I'll tape-record it, so I know how it sounds, and can listen to it over and over in all my darkest hours. Oh, wonderful! Amazing! I never thought I'd see the day!" He spun me around in the corridor. "Oh, what *joy*!"

I had a sudden moment of doubt. Maybe he *wouldn't* hear it. Maybe I couldn't *do* it.

"No!" I told myself sternly. "Don't even *think* about failure. Like Leighton Buzzard Wanderers, it's onwards and upwards!"

And I strolled off, whistling.

When I got home, I added up.

"If I do a quarter past eight till a quarter past three, that will be seven hours."

Mum checked my working.

"And if everyone pays me everything

they've promised, I'll have ten million —"

"Let's leave the dinner ladies out of this," said Mum. "Just for the moment."

"All right then." I added up without them. "Now I'll multiply by seven."

Mum checked my working again.

And there it was. The answer.

"That's *amazing*. With that much, Mrs Heap could buy a whole new floor-to-ceiling bookcase and *fill* it with books. *Couldn't* she?"

Mum tapped her pencil on her teeth.

"Yes," she said thoughtfully. "If you can manage seven whole hours . . ."

8 Fresh Start, Fresh Colours

WHEN FRIDAY CAME, like Leighton Buzzard Wanderers when they made their fresh start, I wore fresh colours. Gran found me a bright yellow shirt to remind me that Silence is Golden. And round the cuffs she embroidered "Ssssssh! Sssssssh!" in little letters so thick and black they looked just like stripes.

"They're to remind you, too."

And then I got the pep talk.

"Listen!" said Mum.

"I am listening."

"No," Mum explained. "That is our strategy for the day. For you to *listen*."

"Listen?"

"Yes," Mum said. "It's a defensive tack. You see, if you're busy listening, then you won't get bored and start talking. And you'll find out what goes on when you're not interrupting all the time. It'll be *interesting*."

"*Interesting?*"

"Yes," she said firmly. "Think about it. You'll be like a fly on the wall, and get to see what things are like without you."

The more I thought about it, the stranger it sounded.

"Fly on the wall?"

"That's right."

"Weird!"

Mum put her finger on her lips. "Remember, if you *talk*, then it won't work. Things will just go back to being how they are usually."

"Like when Leighton Buzzard Wanderers ended up back in the fourth division?"

"That's right. Like that."

"Right," I said. "Match tactic. Fly on the wall. Not talking. *Listening*."

"That's the spirit," Mum told me. She made the Leighton Buzzard Wanderers Victory Salute. "Now go out there, Louis, and win, win, *win*."

9 Interesting . . .

FIRST STOP, THE lollipop crossing. As I
walked closer, Mrs Frier was reaching out
to pull Bernie Henderson back from the
kerb, as usual. On any other morning I
would have begun to chat to her about
something. But instead I lagged behind, in
case she'd forgotten it was a special day,
and asked if the cat had got my tongue.

So she had time, for once, to speak to
Bernie.

"Young man, you practically *hurl*
yourself off that kerb every morning.
Did you know that, for every girl your

age who has a road accident, seven boys get run over?"

"*Seven?*"

Bernie looked really shocked, and stepped right back.

"That's right," said Mrs Frier. "And doesn't that show that charging off the kerb isn't a smart idea?"

She stepped out in the next gap to stop all the traffic. And this time Bernie waited until she gave him the wink before he moved.

Mrs Frier said, as I walked past her: "Hello, Louis. I didn't notice you there, even in that nice bright shirt."

Fly on the wall, see? I gave her the thumbs-up, to show that, although I wasn't speaking, I was still friendly.

"Oh, right!" she said, remembering. "Your sponsored silence! Well, best of luck!"

I nearly said "thank you" and ruined it.

But Bernie interrupted just in time.

"Seven boys! For every girl! It makes you think, doesn't it?"

So that was my first few minutes. I'd heard something interesting from Mrs Frier (and probably saved Bernie Henderson's life).

It was the same in the playground. I kept hearing fascinating things.

"So Moira's mother has to go and
meet the Queen, and wear a fancy hat."

"And when my brother looked at the
apple, he saw half a maggot, waving."

"Oh, yes. Each year the top class go to
Alton Towers."

"Mrs Prenderghast saw a ghost in her
closet."

I wandered round, listening. Behind
the shed, I saw Dora curtsying

beautifully to one of the dustbins, but since she wasn't saying anything, I drifted back to the playground and heard Roberta saying to Amelia, "My dance teacher says if I can't learn to curtsy properly, I can't be one of the Twelve Dancing Princesses in our show."

"Is curtsying hard?" asked Amelia.

"*I* think so," said Roberta. "I get my feet all mixed up. And I can never remember how to start."

I grabbed her hand and tugged. She gave me a funny look and said, "What's the matter, Louis?"

I put my fingers on my lips and shook my head, but kept on tugging.

"He can't talk," Amelia reminded Roberta. "He's on his sponsored silence."

So Roberta let me drag her round behind the shed, and Amelia followed us. And there they saw Dora, curtsying beautifully to the dustbins. Roberta rushed up to copy how she put her feet. Amelia joined in as well. And when I walked away, the three of them were busy making arrangements to meet in break-time for another practice.

And then the bell rang. While we were trooping in for Assembly, Roberta gave my hand a secret squeeze.

"Louis," she whispered. "If I get to be one of the Twelve Dancing Princesses, I'm going to give you my granny's old Read-Easy Magnifying Glass, and that's a promise."

A Read-Easy Magnifying Glass. It sounded good.

Usually, I hate Assembly. The hall's cold, I hate sitting still in boring lines, and it seems to go on for ever. The only part I like is the singing, and by the time we get to that, it's all dragged on so long, we only have time to sing one or two verses.

This time, it was over too soon. I don't know what happened. One minute, Mrs Heap was nattering on as usual about not dropping litter, and noise in the corridors. But because I couldn't just turn to the person next to me and whisper, as usual, I had to stare round quietly.

And that's how I came to notice the second hand on the clock.

I watched it sweep round. When it reached the exact top, I shut my eyes and tried to guess how long a minute was. When I opened my eyes again, thinking I'd see the second hand swooping past the top again, it was still only halfway round.

I tried again.

This time, I was better at guessing. Only twenty seconds out.

The next guess was even closer. I missed by just five seconds.

Then I tried counting. First, I did a
minute's test run, watching the clock and
getting the rhythm right. (After all, being
able to count to a minute without a
watch might come in useful if I ever join

the army or a television company.)

Then, after my test run, I had another go with my eyes closed.

And I was spot on. *Perfect.*

So I did it again, to prove it wasn't just a fluke. And this time I was only one second out, so I counted that as well.

And then, even though I wasn't listening, I heard my name called out by Mrs Heap.

"Louis Todd –"

I looked up, *furious*. I hadn't said *a single word*.

But then I heard the rest.

"– can sing the song along with all the rest of us without spoiling his big silence."

Mrs Heap waved at Mr Hambleton at the piano.

"And since I haven't had to keep stopping this Assembly to tell people off for talking –" (was she looking at *me*?)

"– today we have time to sing every verse!"

Excellent. And Mr Hambleton picked the song that he *knows* is my favourite. *Curious* . . .

I'm not used to sitting quietly through work-time. I kept on nearly cracking. In the end I pretended I'd forgotten what Dad said, and borrowed Bethany's sticky tape. Miss Sparkes pretended not to see me sticking it over my mouth. And we got on with Maths Workbook.

I couldn't talk, so I was forced to listen.

"I can't do subtraction," Bethany was wailing.

"Easy-peasy," said Lyle.

"I'm *stuck*."

Lyle leaned over Bethany's workbook. "You're not stuck. You just have to *borrow*."

"I *hate* borrowing," Bethany grumbled.

"I always get it wrong when I pay back."

I was about to tell Bethany all about the time I got all twenty wrong. But the sticky tape stopped me. So I just had to listen to Lyle explain things to Bethany.

"Have you got it now?"

"Nearly. Just tell me one more time."

So he explained it again, and I still had to listen.

"*Now* do you understand?"

"Yes," said Bethany. "But just tell me the bit about paying back one more time."

So Lyle said it *again*. I nearly peeled off my sticky tape to tell him to shut up. But I didn't. And then Miss Sparkes came and stood over us for ten whole minutes while we got on with it.

And Bethany got every single one of them right.

And so did I.

Interesting . . .

After that, it was Reading Time. Miss Sparkes picked a story about a ghost. Usually, we read in groups. (I'm on the blue table.) But on the day of my big silence, she brought in a big pile of books, and said we'd be reading in turns round the whole class.

"Except for Louis," she said. "Because he can't talk. So he's going to have the ghost's part because going '*Whooo*' doesn't count."

It made a nice rest from the silence, going "*Whooo*".

"Whooo!" I went.

And then, when my next bit came: "Whoooooo!"

And then, in the really scary bit:

"Whoooooooooooooooooooooooooooooooooooo!"

"That was very good," Miss Sparkes said at the end. "Everyone read beautifully, and Louis's wailing was excellent."

I didn't say, "You're welcome." I just grinned. And then, before I could even believe we'd got through a whole story before the bell, it rang for lunch-time.

Interesting . . .

This listening business is even cleverer
than you think. While we were standing
in the queue for lunch, I was the only one
who wasn't talking, so I was the only one
who got to hear that funny sizzling noise.

I turned around.

It was a new tray of macaroni cheese,
fresh from the oven. Brown, bubbling
and hot.

Suzie pushed me forward. (She was
busy chattering to Frances.)

I looked at the cold, claggy yellow
sludge on the tray in front of Mrs Patel.
There were only two squares left.

I nearly made the mistake of saying,
"After you," but stopped just in time.
Instead, I bent down and pretended to
fiddle with my shoe lace.

"Keep the queue moving, girls!" called
Mrs Patel. "Walk round Louis and I'll
serve you."

They didn't realize. They just hurried round, and took the last two claggy squares. I came up after them, and she gave me the first serving out of the sizzling hot brown tray.

"I'm giving you a big one," Mrs Patel said, "because you're doing so well, and everyone's so pleased with you."

(And that's another thing I wouldn't have heard if I had been talking, as usual.)

After lunch, it was Mr Hambleton and Percussion Band. He came in with the tape recorder, looking horribly worried.

Nodding at me, he asked the others, "So how's he doing?"

"Brilliantly!" Caleb said loyally. "He hasn't said a *word*."

Mr Hambleton beamed. "Oh, joy! I *never* thought he'd get this far through the day. I've been chewing my nails all morning. I even tried to get Mrs Heap to let me have you all straight after Assembly. But she said not one of you could afford to miss Maths Workbook."

"I could next week," said Bethany. "Now that I understand borrowing and paying back."

But Mr Hambleton wasn't listening. He was diving into the boxes.

"Quick! Before Louis cracks!" He handed out triangles and woodblocks and castanets. Then he turned to me.

"Don't *speak*!" he warned. "Just point to what you'd like to play today while you keep quiet."

I couldn't believe it. No one in the whole history of Percussion Band has ever got to *choose*.

I stared at all the things I love the best.

The glockenspiel.

The chiming bells.

The marimbas.

The cymbals.

The timpani drum.

I picked the chiming bells.

When we were all set up, Mr Hambleton stood by the tape recorder and made a speech.

"This is a very special day for me," he said. "As you all know, I love music. It is my greatest joy. So it has been a great

strain and a misery to have it ruined
every single week by constant chattering
and interrupting."

(If I hadn't been on a sponsored
silence, I'd have spoken up then, and said
that it wasn't *all* me. But I was, so I
didn't.)

"But today –"

Mr Hambleton's eyes shone and his
voice wobbled. He couldn't carry on. He
was too moved. I felt a little nervous. I'd
had a lot more practice interrupting than
playing on the chiming bells. But, when
we started, it was really very easy. If
you're not talking, you have time to
watch. And then you see him pointing
your way when it's time to get ready. And
when it's time to go, he sweeps you in.

You'd have to be an idiot to get it
wrong.

(Or not really *listening*.)

We played *Surf Song* and *Bell-Time* and

Ghost Walk Rock. Then we swapped
instruments (I chose the cymbals this
time) and carried on. We did *Circus* and
Twilight Time.

"Oh, this is wonderful!" Mr
Hambleton said when the tape clicked at

the end. "We have time to record on the other side."

So we did *Dem Bones, Dem Bones, Punch and Judy* and *Lullaby* before the tape ran out and the bell rang.

"Oh, thank you!" cried Mr Hambleton. "Thank you all!" He clutched the cassette tape to his heart. "I shall *treasure* this," he told us. "*Treasure* it! Thank you to *everyone*. Thank you, Louis! Thank you! Thank you!"

He was still saying it as we trooped out. "Thank you! Oh, thank you!"

Caleb poked me in the ribs and whispered, "That's interesting. Today Mr Hambleton is finding it even harder to keep quiet than you are!"

Then it was time to go and watch *Pictures from History*. I sat next to Geoff (since he was sponsoring me particularly to shut up through that). We chose chairs in the middle of the front row, and I was really glad, because it was *amazing*.

First, they explained about what people did in the days before toilets were invented.

Then they showed a film about a pretty girl who emptied her slops out of her attic window on to the Lord Mayor, and ended up marrying him.

Then they showed us a Potty Museum. (Honestly!) And the curator showed us all his favourites.

And then it ended with some splunky music, and pictures of loos through the ages.

I turned to Geoff and nearly told him, "That was *amazing*." But he clapped his hand over my mouth and stopped me *just in time*.

On the way down to the gym, I had a think. I'll tell you what was on my mind.

I knew that, if anyone else had been trying to be quiet for a whole day, everyone would have been trying to trick them into forgetting.

Not spitefully. Just for fun.

But no one was doing that to me. In fact, they were trying to help me. If they came up, they kept their fingers on their lips, to remind me. And if they passed me notes in class, they wrote *Sssh!* on the top, in case I forgot. And, the whole day, not one single person had come up behind me in the playground and called out, "Hey Louis!" hoping I'd swing round and say, "What?" without thinking.

And I thought I knew why.

It was because they wanted me to do it. They wanted me to get through the day without talking as much as I did.

And not just because they're my friends, but because they were enjoying it. It made a nice change to get through lessons without having to stop all the time for, "Someone is talking. Is it you, Louis?" and, "I'm not carrying on until Louis stops talking."

And that was interesting. It made me think.

We didn't get to climb the ropes in gym. But it wasn't my fault. Miss Hunter wasn't in the mood. She'd planned a ball game, and wasn't going to change it. Not for anyone.

Not even for someone so quiet they heard every whisper. "Louis, quick! No one's marking me. Throw the ball this way!"

So quiet, they heard Wayne say, "This is brilliant! Today Louis is gaining us more points than he's losing from talking, so our team's going to *win*."

So quiet that, when the bell rang, they heard Miss Hunter promise: "If you're all this good next week, we'll have the ropes out. That's a *promise*."

Back in the classroom, before going-home time, we did a bit more work, but then Miss Sparkes stopped us early.

"See this?" she said, rooting in her bag.

"Usually by now, I'm looking for aspirins, but today I'm digging for my peppermints."

Everyone got one. Not just me.

"Don't say 'thank you'," she warned me. "Just keep on going till a quarter past three, and that will make *seven whole hours*."

I could hardly believe it.

They clapped me out, like Leighton Buzzard Wanderers the day they went up in the League.

Dora and Roberta and Amelia all curtsied to me beautifully as I walked by.

The dinner ladies banged their saucepan lids as I went past the kitchens.

Mrs Heap was standing on the steps, browsing through library-plaque catalogues. "We must do this again very soon," she said to me hopefully.

At the kerb, Bernie Henderson stood well back while Mrs Frier stopped the traffic. She raised her lollipop sign in a salute as I walked past.

Mrs Havergill handed a rose to me over the garden wall as I walked up the path. "You might think of keeping going through the weekend," she suggested.

And Gran was waiting at the door.

"*Well,*" she said. "That golden yellow hasn't stood up very well to a long day in school. It looks quite grubby. I think I'm going to have to whip it off you, and put it in the wash, and —"

I wasn't even listening. I was counting the second hand round to the end of the very last minute. (I could have done it with my eyes closed, but it was important to be *sure.*)

Three. Two. One.

YES!!!

And then I spoke.

"I did it! It was brilliant! I had a *great* day! It was *wonderful.* I got to play the

chiming bells, and I understood
borrowing properly, and we read a ghost
story all the way through, and I saw an
amazing film about potties, and –"

The phone rang. It was Mum.

"How did it go?"

"*Amazing!* I saved Bernie Henderson's
life, and fixed things so that Roberta got
a part in her dancing show, and we sang
my favourite song in Assembly, and I
learned to count to a minute without a
watch, and –"

The door flew open. It was Dad, home
early from school.

"How did it go?"

"*Superb!* I found out that next year we
get to go to Alton Towers, and lunch was
the best ever, and our team won the ball
game, and Miss Sparkes gave me a
peppermint, and I've made *millions* for
the new library. *Millions*."

Dad looked a bit wistful. "We need a

new library too," he said. "You wouldn't
think of coming over to be quiet at our
school?"

"No," I said. "No, I wouldn't. But I did
think I might spend a bit more time
being quiet in my own."

10 Fly on the Wall

AND SO I have. Not terribly quiet, and not all the time. But just enough.

Everyone's happier. They all paid up (except for the dinner ladies, who tried to pretend that their noughts were just fancy decoration. But, to make up, they have lent Mr Hambleton a bit of serving counter for tapes of *The Percussion Band Medley*. And sales of that are going really well, so we'll probably get to ten million without them.)

And the new library's open. People still go round boasting about how they raised money for it. How they washed cars, or made biscuits, or had wet sponges thrown at them, or sold raffle tickets. Even Miss Sparkes is still bragging about making five whole pounds by auctioning the timer that never worked on me.

"What made you change, anyway?" she keeps on asking.

But I won't say. I won't give any clues. ("That's the spirit!" says Mum. "Be like Leighton Buzzard Wanderers and keep your secrets.") But sometimes, just sometimes, I see Miss Sparkes watching me grinning at some fly on the wall, and I wonder if she guesses.

Nobody calls me Mr Loudmouth any more. Not that I'm totally silent. I still talk a little more than most.

But hardly ever in class, when we're trying to get work done.

And never in Percussion Band, except between pieces.

And never, ever when I'm in the

library, sitting next to Bernie Henderson
(who, thanks to me, is still alive) and
reading through Roberta's granny's old
Read-Easy Magnifying Glass.

In my favourite place. Under the
plaque that says *Silence was Golden*.